The Wonderful Wizard of Oz

L. Frank Baum

Condensed and Adapted by
SUZI ALEXANDER

Illustrated by
NICK PRICE

Cover Illustrated by
MARK ELLIOTT

bendon

The Junior Classics have been
adapted and illustrated with care and thought
to introduce you to a world of famous authors, characters, ideas,
and great stories that have been loved for generations.

Editor — Kathryn Knight
Creative Director — Gina Rhodes Haynes
And the entire classics project team
of Bendon Publishing

THE WONDERFUL WIZARD OF OZ

Copyright © 2014
Bendon Publishing International, Inc.
Ashland, Ohio 44805 • 1-888-5-BENDON
bendonpub.com

Printed in the United States of America

A note to the reader—

A classic story rests in your hands. The characters are famous. The tale is timeless.

This Junior Classic edition of *The Wonderful Wizard of Oz* has been carefully condensed and adapted from the original version (which you really *must* read when you're ready for every detail). We kept the well-known phrases for you. We kept Lyman Frank Baum's style. And we kept the important imagery and heart of the tale.

Literature is terrific fun! It encourages you to think. It helps you dream. It is full of heroes and villains, suspense and humor, adventure and wonder, and new ideas. It introduces you to writers who reach out across time to say: "Do you want to hear a story I wrote?"

Curl up and enjoy.

CONTENTS

CHARACTERS

DOROTHY — a little girl from the prairies of Kansas, who finds herself in the Land of Oz

UNCLE HENRY AND AUNT EM — Dorothy's Uncle and Aunt

TOTO — Dorothy's little black dog

THE MUNCHKINS — odd little people who live in the East of Oz

THE GOOD WITCH OF THE NORTH — the kind witch from the North of Oz

THE WICKED WITCH OF THE EAST — the bad witch in the East of Oz, killed by Dorothy's house

THE SCARECROW — Dorothy's new friend who seeks a Brain from the Wizard

THE TIN WOODMAN — Dorothy's new friend who seeks a Heart from the Wizard

THE COWARDLY LION — Dorothy's new friend who seeks Courage from the Wizard

THE QUEEN OF THE FIELD MICE — the new friend who comes to Dorothy's aid

THE GUARDIAN OF THE GATES — the doorkeeper of the Emerald City of Oz

THE GREAT AND TERRIBLE OZ — the Wizard who rules over the Land of Oz

THE WICKED WITCH OF THE WEST — the bad witch who rules over the Winkies in the West of Oz

THE WINGED MONKEYS — flying monkeys who obey the wearer of the Golden Cap

THE WINKIES — the people who live in the West of Oz

THE HAMMER-HEADS — flat-headed men with an odd way of doing battle

THE QUADLINGS — the people who live in the South of Oz

GLINDA, THE GOOD WITCH OF THE SOUTH — the kind witch who rules over the Quadlings

The Wonderful Wizard of Oz

CHAPTER ONE

The Cyclone

Dorothy lived in the midst of the great Kansas prairies with Uncle Henry, who was a farmer, Aunt Em, who was the farmer's wife, and Toto, who was a little black dog that Dorothy loved dearly. Their house was small (for the lumber to build it had to be carried by wagon many miles). There were four walls, a floor and a roof, which made one room. There was no storage area at all, and no cellar—except a small hole dug in the ground, called a cyclone cellar, where the family could go in case a mighty whirlwind arose. It was reached by a trap door in the middle of the floor. A ladder led down into the small, dark hole.

Today, Uncle Henry sat upon the doorstep and looked anxiously at the sky, which was even grayer than usual. Dorothy stood in the door with Toto in her arms and looked at the sky, too. Aunt Em was washing the dishes.

From the far north they heard a low wail of the wind, and Uncle Henry and Dorothy could see where the long grass bowed in waves before the coming storm.

Suddenly Uncle Henry stood up.

"There's a cyclone coming, Em," he called to his wife.

"Quick, Dorothy!" Aunt Em screamed. "Run for the cellar!"

Toto jumped out of Dorothy's arms and hid under the bed, and the girl started to get him. Aunt Em, badly frightened, threw open the trap door in the floor and climbed down the ladder into the small, dark hole. Dorothy caught Toto at last and started to follow her aunt. When Dorothy was halfway across the room there came a great shriek from the wind, and the house shook so hard that she lost her footing and sat down suddenly upon the floor.

Then a strange thing happened.

The house whirled around two or three times and rose slowly through the air. Dorothy felt as if she were going up in a balloon.

It was very dark, and the wind howled horribly around her, but Dorothy found she was riding quite easily. After the first few whirls around, she felt as if she were being rocked gently, like a baby in a cradle.

In spite of the swaying of the house and the wailing of the wind, Dorothy soon closed her eyes and fell fast asleep.

CHAPTER TWO

The Council with the Munchkins

She was awakened by a *thud!* so sudden that if Dorothy had not been lying on the soft bed she might have been hurt. The shock made her catch her breath and Toto put his cold little nose into her face and whined sadly. Dorothy sat up and noticed that the house was not moving. Nor was it dark, for the bright sunshine came in at the window, flooding the little room. She sprang from her bed and, with Toto at her heels, ran and opened the door.

The cyclone had set the house down very gently (for a cyclone) in the midst of a country of marvelous beauty. There were lovely patches

of green earth all about, with stately trees bearing rich and delicious fruits. Gorgeous flowers were everywhere, and pretty birds with colorful feathers sang and fluttered in the trees and bushes.

While she stood looking eagerly at the strange and beautiful sights, she noticed coming toward her a group of the oddest people she had ever seen. They were not as big as the grown folk she had always been used to, but neither were they very small. In fact, they seemed about as tall as Dorothy, who was a well-grown child for her age.

Three were men and one was a woman, and all were oddly dressed. They wore round hats that rose to a small point a foot above their heads, with little bells around the brims that tinkled sweetly as they moved. The men, Dorothy thought, were about as old as Uncle Henry, for two of them had beards. But the little woman was much older.

These people drew near the house where Dorothy was standing in the doorway.

The little old woman walked up to Dorothy, made a low bow and said, in a sweet voice, "You are welcome to the land of the Munchkins. We are so grateful to you for having killed the Wicked Witch of the East and for setting our people free."

Dorothy said slowly, "You are very kind, but there must be some mistake. I have not killed anything."

"Your house did, anyway," replied the little old woman, with a laugh, "and that is the same thing. See!" She pointed to the corner of the house. "There are her two feet, still sticking out from under a block of wood."

Dorothy looked and gave a little cry of fright. There, indeed, just under the corner of the

house, were two feet sticking out—wearing silver shoes with pointed toes.

"Oh, dear! Oh, dear!" cried Dorothy, clasping her hands together in dismay. "The house must have fallen on her. Whatever shall we do?"

"There is nothing to be done," said the little woman calmly.

"But who was she?" asked Dorothy.

"She was the Wicked Witch of the East, as I said," answered the little woman. "She has held all the Munchkins in captivity for many years, making them slave for her night and day. Now they are all set free, and they are grateful to you for the favor."

"Who are the Munchkins?" inquired Dorothy.

"They are the people who live in this land of the East, where the Wicked Witch ruled."

"Are you a Munchkin?" asked Dorothy.

"No, but I am their friend, although I live in the land of the North. When they saw the Witch of the East was dead, the Munchkins sent a swift messenger to me, and I came at once. I am the Witch of the North."

"Oh, gracious!" cried Dorothy. "Are you a real witch?"

"Yes, indeed," answered the little woman. "But I am a good witch, and the people love me. I am not as powerful as the Wicked Witch was who ruled here, or I would have set the people free myself."

Dorothy was going to ask another question, but just then the Munchkins, who had been standing silently by, gave a loud shout and pointed to the corner of the house where the Wicked Witch had been lying.

"What is it?" asked the little old woman. She looked and began to laugh. The feet of the dead Witch had disappeared, and nothing was left but the silver shoes.

"She was so old," explained the Witch of the North, "that she dried up quickly in the sun. That is the end of her. But the Silver Shoes are yours, and you shall have them to wear." She reached down, picked up the shoes, and, after shaking the dust out of them, handed them to Dorothy.

"The Witch of the East was proud of those Silver Shoes," said one of the Munchkins, "and they have a magic charm, but we don't know what it is."

Dorothy took off her old leather shoes and

tried on the silver ones, which fit her as well as if they had been made for her.

"I am anxious to get back to my aunt and uncle, for I am sure they will worry about me. Can you help me find my way?"

"You must go to the City of Emeralds," said the Witch of the North. "Perhaps Oz will help you."

"Where is this city?" asked Dorothy.

"It is exactly in the center of the country. It is ruled by Oz, the Great Wizard."

"Is he a good man?" inquired the girl anxiously.

"He is a good Wizard. Whether he is a man or not I cannot tell, for I have never seen him."

"How can I get there?" asked Dorothy.

"You must walk. It is a long journey, through a country that is sometimes pleasant and sometimes dark and terrible. However, I will use all the magic I know to keep you from harm."

"Won't you go with me?" pleaded the girl, who had begun to look upon the little old woman as her only friend.

"No, I cannot do that," she replied, "but I will give you my kiss, and no one will dare injure a person who has been kissed by the Witch of the North."

She came close to Dorothy and kissed her gently on the forehead. Where her lips touched the girl they left a round, shining mark, as Dorothy found out soon after.

"The road to the City of Emeralds is paved with yellow brick," said the Witch, "so you cannot miss it. When you get to Oz do not be afraid of him, but tell your story and ask him to help you. Good-bye, my dear."

CHAPTER THREE

How Dorothy Saved the Scarecrow

Dorothy had only one other dress which was hanging on a peg beside her bed. It had checks of white and blue. It was somewhat faded with many washings, yet it was still a pretty frock. So, Dorothy went back into the house, washed herself carefully, dressed herself in the clean dress, and tied her pink sunbonnet on her head. She took a little basket and filled it with bread from the cupboard, laying a white cloth over the top.

"Come along, Toto," she said. "We will go to the Emerald City and ask the Great Oz how to get back to Kansas again."

There were several roads nearby, but it did not take her long to find the one paved with yellow bricks. Within a short time she was walking briskly toward the Emerald City, her Silver Shoes tinkling merrily on the hard, yellow road.

When she had gone several miles, she thought she would stop to rest. She climbed to the top of the fence beside the road and sat down. There was a great cornfield beyond the fence, and not far away she saw a Scarecrow placed high on a pole to keep the birds from the ripe corn.

Dorothy leaned her chin upon her hand and gazed thoughtfully at the Scarecrow. Its head was a small sack stuffed with straw, with eyes, nose, and mouth painted on for the face. An old, pointed Munchkin hat was perched on its head. The rest of the body was a blue suit of clothes, worn and faded, which had also been stuffed with straw. On the feet were some old boots with blue tops. The Scarecrow was raised above the stalks of corn on a pole stuck up its back.

While Dorothy was looking into the odd, painted face of the Scarecrow, she was surprised to see one of the eyes slowly wink at her. She thought she must have been mistaken at first, for none of the scarecrows in Kansas ever wink. Yet then the figure nodded its head to her in a friendly way. She climbed down from the fence and walked up to it, while Toto ran around the pole and barked.

"Good day," said the Scarecrow huskily.

"Did you *speak?*" asked the girl in wonder.

"Certainly," answered the Scarecrow. "How do you do?"

"I'm pretty well, thank you," replied Dorothy politely. "How do *you* do?"

"I'm not feeling well," said the Scarecrow with a smile, "for it is very difficult being perched up here night and day to scare away crows."

"Can't you get down?" asked Dorothy.

"No, for this pole is stuck up my back. If you will please take away the pole I shall be greatly thankful."

Dorothy reached up both arms and lifted him off the pole, for, being stuffed with straw, he was quite light.

"Thank you very much," said the Scarecrow, when he had been set down on the ground. "I feel like a new man. But tell me—who are you? And where are you going?"

"My name is Dorothy," said the girl, "and I am going to the Emerald City to ask the Great Oz to send me back to Kansas."

"Where is the Emerald City?" he asked. "And who is Oz?"

"Why, don't you know?" she returned, in surprise.

"No, indeed. I don't know anything. You see, I am stuffed, so I have no brains at all," he answered sadly.

"Oh," said Dorothy, "I'm awfully sorry for you."

"Do you think," he asked, "if I go to the Emerald City with you, that Oz would give me some brains?"

"I cannot tell," she returned, "but you may come with me, if you like. If Oz will not give you any brains you will be no worse off than you are now."

"Thank you," he answered gratefully.

They walked back to the road. Dorothy helped him over the fence and they started along the path of yellow brick for the Emerald City.

CHAPTER FOUR

The Rescue of the Tin Woodman

After a few hours the road began to be rough. The walking grew so difficult that the Scarecrow often stumbled over the yellow bricks, which were very uneven. Sometimes, indeed, they were broken or missing altogether, leaving holes that Toto jumped across and Dorothy walked around. As for the Scarecrow, having no brains, he walked straight ahead, and so stepped into the holes and fell at full length on the hard bricks. It never hurt him, however, and Dorothy would pick him up and set him upon his feet again, while he joined her in laughing merrily at his own mishap.

Suddenly, they were startled to hear a deep groan nearby.

"What was that?" Dorothy asked timidly.

"I cannot imagine," replied the Scarecrow, "but we can go and see."

Just then another groan reached their ears, and the sound seemed to come from behind them. They turned and had walked through the forest a few steps when Dorothy discovered something shining in a ray of sunshine that fell between the trees. She ran to the place and then stopped short with a little cry of surprise.

One of the big trees had been partly chopped through, and standing beside it, with an axe in his hands, was a man made entirely of tin. His head and arms and legs were jointed upon his body, but he stood perfectly still, as if he could not move at all.

"Did you groan?" asked Dorothy.

"Yes," answered the tin man, "I did. I've been groaning for more than a year, and no one has ever heard me before or come to help me."

"What can I do for you?" she inquired softly.

"Get my oil can and oil my joints," he answered. "They are rusted so badly that

I cannot move them at all."

Dorothy found the oil can, and asked anxiously, "Where are your joints?"

"Oil my neck first," replied the Tin Woodman.

So she did, while the Scarecrow moved the head gently from side to side.

"Then oil the joints in my arms," he said. Dorothy oiled them and the Scarecrow bent

them carefully until they were quite free from rust and as good as new. Then they oiled his leg joints and he was able to move about.

"This is a great comfort," he said. "I have been holding that axe in the air ever since I rusted, and I'm glad to be able to put it down at last. I might have stood there forever if you had not come along, so you have certainly saved my life. How did you happen to be here?"

"We are on our way to the Emerald City to see the Great Oz," Dorothy answered.

"Why do you wish to see Oz?" he asked.

"I want him to send me back to Kansas, and the Scarecrow wants him to put a few brains into his head," she replied.

The Tin Woodman appeared to think deeply for a moment. Then he said, "Do you suppose Oz could give me a heart?"

"Why, I guess so," Dorothy answered. "It would be as easy as to give the Scarecrow brains."

"True," the Tin Woodman said. "So, if you will allow me to join you, I will also go to the Emerald City and ask Oz to help me."

"Come along," said the Scarecrow heartily, and Dorothy added that she would be pleased

to have his company. So the Tin Woodman shouldered his axe and they all passed through the forest until they came to the road that was paved with yellow brick.

The Tin Woodman had asked Dorothy to put the oil can in her basket. "For," he said, "if I should get caught in the rain, and should rust again, I would need the oil can badly."

CHAPTER FIVE

The Cowardly Lion

"How long will it be," the child asked of the Tin Woodman, "before we are out of the forest?"

"I cannot tell," was the answer, "for I have never been to the Emerald City. But my father went there once, when I was a boy. He said it was a long journey through a dangerous country, although nearer to the city where Oz dwells the country is beautiful. But I am not afraid so long as I have my oil can, and nothing can hurt the Scarecrow. You have the mark of the Good Witch's kiss on your forehead, and that will protect *you* from harm."

Just as he spoke, there came from the forest a

terrible roar. The next moment, a great Lion bounded into the road. With one blow of his paw he sent the Scarecrow spinning over and over to the edge of the road, and then he struck at the Tin Woodman with his sharp claws and the Woodman fell over in the road and lay still.

Little Toto, now that he had an enemy to face, ran barking toward the Lion. The great beast had opened his mouth to bite the dog when Dorothy, fearing Toto would be killed, rushed forward and slapped the Lion upon his nose as hard as she could. She cried out, "Don't you dare bite Toto! You ought to be ashamed of yourself, a big beast like you, trying to bite a poor little dog!"

"I didn't bite him," said the Lion. He rubbed his nose with his paw where Dorothy had hit it.

"No, but you tried to," she retorted. "You are nothing but a big coward."

"I know it," said the Lion, hanging his head in shame. "I've always known it."

"But that isn't right. The King of Beasts shouldn't be a coward," said the Scarecrow.

"I know it," returned the Lion, wiping a tear from his eye with the tip of his tail. "It is my great sorrow, and makes my life very unhappy.

For whenever there is danger, my heart begins to beat fast."

"Perhaps you have heart disease," said the Tin Woodman.

"It may be," said the Lion.

"If you have," continued the Tin Woodman, "you ought to be glad, for it proves you have a heart. For my part, I have no heart, so I cannot have heart disease."

"Perhaps," said the Lion thoughtfully, "if I had no heart I would not be a coward."

"Have you brains?" asked the Scarecrow.

"I suppose so. I've never looked to see," replied the Lion.

"I am going to the Great Oz to ask him to give me some," remarked the Scarecrow, "for my head is stuffed with straw."

"And I am going to ask him to give me a heart," said the Woodman.

"And I am going to ask him to send Toto and me back to Kansas," added Dorothy.

"Do you think Oz could give me courage?" asked the Cowardly Lion.

"Just as easily as he could give me brains," said the Scarecrow.

"Or give me a heart," said the Tin Woodman.

"Or send me back to Kansas," said Dorothy.

"Then, if you don't mind, I'll go with you," said the Lion, "for my life is simply unbearable without a bit of courage."

"You will be very welcome," answered Dorothy, "for you will help to keep away the other wild beasts. It seems to me they must be more cowardly than you are if they allow you to scare them so easily."

So once more the little company set off upon the journey, the Lion walking with stately strides at Dorothy's side.

CHAPTER SIX

The Journey to the Great Oz

The day that followed was to be an eventful one for Dorothy and her fellow travelers. They had hardly been walking an hour when they saw before them a great ditch that crossed the road and divided the forest as far as they could see on either side.

"What shall we do?" asked Dorothy in despair.

"I think I could jump over it," said the Cowardly Lion, after measuring the distance carefully in his mind.

"Then we are all right," answered the Scarecrow, "for you can carry us all over on your back, one at a time."

The Scarecrow sat upon the Lion's back, and the big beast walked to the edge of the gulf and crouched down. Then giving a great spring, the Lion shot through the air and landed safely on the other side. They were all greatly pleased to see how easily he did it. The Scarecrow got off, and the Lion sprang across the ditch again.

Dorothy thought she would go next, so she took Toto in her arms and climbed onto the Lion's back, holding tightly to his mane with one hand. The next moment it seemed as if she were flying through the air, and then, before she had time to think about it, she was safe on the other side.

The Lion went back a third time and got the Tin Woodman.

They found the forest very thick on this side, and it looked dark and gloomy.

After the Lion had rested, they started along the road of yellow brick, silently wondering, each in his own mind, if ever they would come to the end of the woods and reach the bright sunshine again. To their great joy the trees became thinner the farther they advanced, and they suddenly came upon a broad river, flowing swiftly just before them. On the other side of the water they could see the road of yellow brick running through a beautiful country.

"How shall we cross the river?" asked Dorothy.

"That is easily done," replied the Scarecrow. "The Tin Woodman must build us a raft, so we can float to the other side."

So the Woodman took his axe and began to chop down small trees to make a raft.

When the raft was nearly done, and after the Tin Woodman had cut a few more logs and fastened them together with wooden pins, they were ready to start. The Scarecrow and the Tin Woodman stood upon either end of the raft to steady it. They had long poles in their hands to push the raft through the water.

They got along quite well at first, but when they reached the middle of the river the swift current swept the raft downstream, farther and farther away from the road of yellow brick. The water grew so deep that the long poles would not touch the bottom.

"This is bad," said the Tin Woodman, "for if we cannot get to the land we shall be carried into the country of the Wicked Witch of the West, and she will put a spell on us and make us her slaves."

"We must certainly get to the Emerald City if we can," the Scarecrow added, and he pushed so hard on his long pole that it stuck fast in the mud at the bottom of the river. Then, before he could pull it out again—or let go—the raft was swept away, and the poor Scarecrow was left clinging to the pole in the middle of the river.

Of course, this was a bad thing for the Scarecrow.

"I am now worse off than when I first met Dorothy," he thought. "Then, I was stuck on a pole in a cornfield, where I could make-believe scare the crows, at any rate. But surely there is no use for a Scarecrow stuck on a pole in the middle of a river. I am afraid I shall never have any brains, after all!"

Down the stream the raft floated, and the poor Scarecrow was left far behind. The Lion said in earnest, "Something must be done to save us. I think I can swim to the shore and pull the raft after me, if you will only hold fast to the tip of my tail."

So he sprang into the water, and the Tin Woodman caught fast hold of his tail. Then the Lion began to swim with all his might toward the shore. It was hard work, but by and by they were drawn out of the current.

They were all tired out when they reached the shore at last and stepped off upon the pretty, green grass, and they also knew that the stream had carried them a long way past the road of yellow brick that led to the Emerald City.

Then they all looked at the river and saw the Scarecrow perched upon his pole in the middle of the water, looking very lonely and sad.

"What can we do to save him?" asked Dorothy.

The Lion and the Woodman both shook their heads, for they did not know. So they sat down upon the bank and gazed wistfully at the Scarecrow until a Stork flew by, who, upon seeing them, stopped to rest at the water's edge.

"What are you doing here?" asked the Stork.

"We have lost the Scarecrow, and are wondering how we shall get him again," answered Dorothy.

"Where is he?" asked the Stork.

"Over there in the river," answered the little girl.

"If he wasn't so big and heavy I would get him for you," remarked the Stork.

"He isn't heavy a bit," said Dorothy eagerly, "for he is stuffed with straw!"

"Well, I'll try," said the Stork, "but if I find he is too heavy to carry I shall have to drop him in the river again."

So the big bird flew into the air and over the water till she came to where the Scarecrow was perched upon his pole. Then the Stork, with her

great claws, grabbed the Scarecrow by the arm and carried him up into the air and back to the bank.

When the Scarecrow found himself among his friends again, he was so happy that he hugged them all, even the Lion and Toto.

"Thank you," said Dorothy to the kind Stork, who flew into the air and was soon out of sight.

They walked along, listening to the singing of the brightly-colored birds and looking at the lovely flowers which now became so thick that the ground was carpeted with them. There were big yellow and white and blue and purple blossoms, besides great clusters of scarlet poppies, which were so brilliant in color they almost dazzled Dorothy's eyes.

"Aren't they beautiful?" the girl asked, as she breathed in the spicy scent of the bright flowers.

They now came upon more and more of the big scarlet poppies. It is well known that when there are many of these flowers together their odor is so powerful that anyone who breathes it falls fast asleep, sometimes sleeping on and on forever. But Dorothy did not know this, nor could she get away from the bright red flowers that were everywhere. Her eyes grew heavy. She lay down among the flowers to rest—and was soon asleep.

"What shall we do?" asked the Tin Woodman.

"If we leave her here she will die," said the Lion. "The smell of the flowers is killing us all. I myself can scarcely keep my eyes open, and the dog is asleep already."

It was true. Toto had fallen down beside his little mistress. But the Scarecrow and the Tin Woodman were not troubled by the scent of the flowers.

"Run fast," said the Scarecrow to the Lion, "and get out of this deadly flower bed as soon as you can. We can bring the little girl with us, but if *you* should fall asleep you would be too big to be carried."

So, the Lion bounded forward as the Scarecrow and Tin Woodman carried the sleeping girl and her dog between them through the flowers.

On and on they walked, and it seemed that the great carpet of deadly flowers that surrounded them would never end. They followed the river, and at last came upon their friend the Lion, lying fast asleep among the poppies. The flowers had been too strong for the huge beast and he had given up at last. He had fallen only a short distance from the end of the poppy bed, where the sweet grass spread in beautiful green fields before them.

"We can do nothing for him," said the Tin Woodman sadly, "for he is much too heavy to lift.

We must leave him here to sleep on forever, and perhaps he will dream that he has found courage at last."

They carried the sleeping girl to a pretty spot beside the river, far enough from the poppy field to prevent her from breathing any more of the poison of the flowers. Here they laid her gently on the soft grass and waited for the fresh breeze to wake her.

CHAPTER SEVEN

The Queen of the Field Mice

"We cannot be far from the road of yellow brick, now," remarked the Scarecrow, as he stood beside the girl, "for we have come nearly as far as the river carried us away."

The Tin Woodman was about to reply when he heard a low growl. Turning his head, he saw a strange beast come bounding over the grass toward them. It was, indeed, a great yellow Wildcat. The Woodman thought it must be chasing something, for its ears were lying close to its head and its mouth was wide open, showing two rows of ugly teeth. Its red eyes glowed like balls of fire.

As it came nearer, the Tin Woodman saw the beast was chasing a little gray field mouse. Although the Tin Woodman had no heart, he knew it was wrong for the Wildcat to kill such a pretty, harmless creature. So the Woodman raised his axe and killed the Wildcat.

"Oh, thank you!" said the field mouse in a squeaky little voice. "Thank you ever so much for saving my life."

"Don't speak of it, I beg of you," replied the Woodman. "I have no heart, you know, so I am careful to help all those who may need a friend, even if it happens to be only a mouse."

"Only a mouse!" cried the little animal. "Why, I am a Queen—the Queen of all the Field Mice!"

"Oh, indeed," said the Woodman, making a bow.

"Therefore, you have done a great deed, as well as a brave one, in saving my life," added the Queen.

At that moment several mice ran up as fast as their little legs could carry them.

"Oh, your Majesty, we thought you would be killed! How did you manage to escape the great Wildcat?" and they all bowed so low to the little Queen that they almost stood upon their heads.

"This funny tin man killed the Wildcat," she answered, "and saved my life."

Suddenly, the mice scampered away, for Toto had awakened from his sleep. Seeing all these mice around him, he gave one bark of delight and jumped right into the middle of the group.

But the Tin Woodman caught the dog in his arms and held him tight. He called to the mice, "Come back! Come back! Toto will not hurt you."

The Queen of the Field Mice stuck her head out from a clump of grass and asked timidly, "Are you sure he will not bite us?"

"I will not let him," said the Woodman, "so do not be afraid."

One by one the mice came creeping back, and Toto did not bark again.

One of the biggest mice spoke. "Is there anything we can do to repay you for saving the life of our Queen?"

"Nothing that I know of," replied the Woodman.

The Scarecrow, who had been trying to think, but could not because his head was stuffed with straw, said quickly, "Oh, yes! You can save our friend, the Cowardly Lion, who is asleep in the poppy bed."

"A Lion!" cried the little Queen. "Why, he would eat us all up."

"Oh, no," declared the Scarecrow. "He would never hurt anyone who is our friend. If you will help us to save him, I promise that he shall treat you all with kindness."

"Very well," said the Queen, "we trust you. But what shall we do?"

"Are there many of these mice which call you Queen and are willing to obey you?"

"Oh, yes! There are thousands," she replied.

"Then send for them all to come here as soon as possible, and let each one bring a long piece of string."

The Queen turned to the mice and told them to go at once and get all of her subjects.

"Now," said the Scarecrow to the Tin Woodman, "you must go to those trees by the riverside and make a truck that will carry the Lion."

So the Woodman went at once to the trees and began to work. Soon he made a truck out of the limbs of trees.

The mice came from all directions, and there were thousands of them—big mice and little mice and middle-sized mice. Each one brought a piece of string in his mouth.

It was about this time that Dorothy woke from her long sleep and opened her eyes. She was greatly astonished to find herself lying upon the grass, with thousands of mice standing around and looking at her timidly. But the Scarecrow told her about everything, and turning to the dignified little Mouse, he said, "Permit me to introduce to you Her Majesty, the Queen."

Dorothy nodded and the Queen made a curtsy, after which she became quite friendly with the little girl.

After a great deal of hard work, the Scarecrow and the Woodman pulled the heavy Lion up onto the truck. Then they fastened the mice to the truck, using the strings they had brought.

At first the little mice could hardly stir the heavily loaded truck. The Woodman and the Scarecrow both pushed from behind, and they got along better. Soon they rolled the Lion out of the poppy bed to the green fields, where he could breathe the sweet, fresh air again.

Dorothy came to meet them and thanked the little mice warmly for saving her companion from death. She had grown so fond of the big Lion she was glad he had been rescued.

Then the mice were unharnessed from the truck and they scampered away through the grass to their homes. The Queen of the Field Mice was the last to leave.

"If ever you need us again," she said, "come out into the field and blow upon this whistle, and we shall hear you and come to your assistance. Good-bye!"

"Good-bye!" they all answered. And away the Queen ran, while Dorothy held Toto tightly lest he should run after her and frighten her.

After this they sat down beside the Lion until he awakened. When he did open his eyes and roll off the truck, he was very glad to find himself still alive. Then his friends told him of the field mice, and how they had saved him.

The Lion laughed. "I have always thought myself very big and terrible. Yet such small things as flowers almost killed me. And such small animals as mice have saved my life. How strange it all is!"

Once the Lion was fully refreshed, and feeling quite himself again, they all started upon the journey, greatly enjoying the walk through the soft, fresh grass. It was not long before they reached the road of yellow brick and turned again toward the Emerald City, where the Great Oz lived.

CHAPTER EIGHT

The Guardian of the Gates

They soon saw a beautiful green glow in the sky just before them.

"That must be the Emerald City," said Dorothy.

As they walked on, the green glow became brighter and brighter, and it seemed that at last they were nearing the end of their travels. They soon came to the great wall that surrounded the City. It was high and thick and of a bright green color.

In front of them, and at the end of the road of yellow brick, was a big gate, all studded with emeralds. They glittered so in the sun that even the painted eyes of the Scarecrow were dazzled by their brilliance.

There was a bell beside the gate, and Dorothy pushed the button and heard a silvery tinkle sound within. Then the big gate swung slowly open. They all passed through and found themselves in a high, arched room with walls of glittering emeralds.

Before them stood a little man about the same size as the Munchkins. He was clothed all in green, from his head to his feet, and even his skin was of a greenish tint.

When he saw Dorothy and her companions, the man asked, "What do you wish in the Emerald City?"

"We came to see the Great Oz," said Dorothy.

The man was so surprised at this answer that he sat down to think it over.

"It has been many years since anyone asked me to see Oz," he said, shaking his head. "He is powerful and terrible, and if you come on a foolish errand to bother the Great Wizard, he might be angry and destroy you all in an instant."

"But it is not a foolish errand," replied the Scarecrow. "It is important. And we have been told that Oz is a good Wizard."

"So he is," said the green man, "and he rules the Emerald City wisely and well. But to those who are not honest, or who approach him from curiosity, he is most terrible. Few have ever dared ask to see his face. I am the Guardian of the Gates—and since you demand to see the Great Oz I must take you to his Palace. But first you shall put on eyeglasses."

"Why?" asked Dorothy.

"Because if you did not wear eyeglasses the brightness and glory of the Emerald City would blind you."

He opened a big box that was filled with green-tinted eyeglasses of all sizes and shapes. He fitted them all with a pair—even Toto.

Then the Guardian of the Gates put on his own glasses and told them he was ready to show them to the Palace. Taking a big golden key from a peg on the wall, he opened another gate, and they all followed him into the streets of the Emerald City.

CHAPTER NINE

The Wonderful Emerald City of Oz

Even with the green glasses, Dorothy and her friends were at first dazzled by the wonderful City. All the beautiful houses glittered with emeralds and the road was of shiny green marble. There were many people going to and fro between sparkly shops—shops for green candy, green shoes, green hats, and green clothes.

The Guardian of the Gates led them through the streets until they came to a big building, exactly in the middle of the City, which was the Palace of Oz, the Great Wizard. There was a soldier before the door, dressed in a green uniform and wearing a long, green beard.

"Here are strangers," said the Guardian of the Gates to him, "and they demand to see the Great Oz."

"Step inside," answered the soldier, "and I will carry your message to him."

So they passed through the Palace Gates and were led into a big room with a green carpet and lovely green furniture set with emeralds. The soldier made them all wipe their feet upon a green mat before entering this room, and when

they were seated he said politely, "Please make yourselves comfortable while I go to the door of the Throne Room and tell Oz you are here."

They had to wait a long time before the soldier returned. When, at last, he came back, Dorothy asked, "Have you seen Oz?"

"Oh, no," returned the soldier, "I have never seen him. But I spoke to him as he sat behind his screen and gave him your message. He said he will grant you an audience, if you so desire, but you must wait until tomorrow to enter his presence. Therefore, as you must remain in the Palace, I will have you shown to rooms where you may rest in comfort after your journey."

"Thank you," replied the girl, "that is very kind of Oz."

The soldier now blew upon a green whistle, and at once a young girl, dressed in a pretty green silk gown, entered the room. She had lovely green hair and green eyes, and she bowed low before Dorothy as she said, "Follow me and I will show you your room."

The next morning, after breakfast, the green maiden came to fetch Dorothy and dressed her in one of the prettiest gowns, made of green satin.

Dorothy put on a green silk apron and tied a green ribbon around Toto's neck, and they started for the Throne Room of the Great Oz.

They waited in a great hall until a bell rang. The green girl said to Dorothy, "That is the signal. You must go into the Throne Room alone."

She opened a little door and Dorothy walked boldly through and found herself in a wonderful place. It was a big, round room with a high, arched roof, and the walls and ceiling and floor were covered with large emeralds set closely together. In the center of the roof was a great light, as bright as the sun, which made the emeralds sparkle in a wonderful manner.

But what interested Dorothy most was the big throne of green marble that stood in the middle of the room. It was shaped like a chair and sparkled with gems, as did everything else. In the center of the chair was an enormous Head, without a body to support it or any arms or legs whatsoever. There was no hair upon this Head, but it had eyes and a nose and mouth, and was much bigger than the head of the biggest giant.

As Dorothy gazed upon this in wonder and fear, she heard a voice say:

"I am Oz, the Great and Terrible. Who are you, and why do you seek me?"

It was not such an awful voice as she had expected to come from the big Head. So she took courage and answered, "I am Dorothy, the Small and Meek. I have come to you for help."

The eyes looked at her thoughtfully for a full minute. Then said the voice:

"Where did you get the Silver Shoes?"

"I got them from the Wicked Witch of the East, when my house fell on her and killed her," she replied.

"Where did you get the mark upon your forehead?" continued the voice.

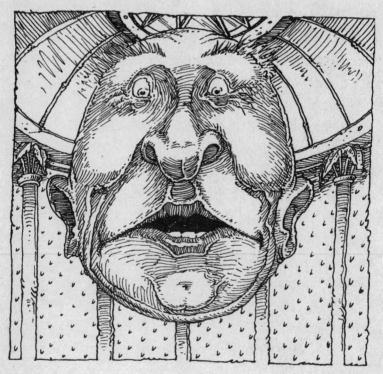

"That is where the Good Witch of the North kissed me when she said good-bye and sent me to you," said the girl.

Again the eyes looked at her sharply, and they saw she was telling the truth. Then Oz asked, "What do you wish me to do?"

"Send me back to Kansas, where my Aunt Em and Uncle Henry are," she answered earnestly.

"Why should I do this for you?" asked Oz.

"Because you are strong and I am weak; because you are a Great Wizard and I am only a little girl."

"But you were strong enough to kill the Wicked Witch of the East," said Oz.

"That just happened," returned Dorothy simply. "I could not help it."

"Well," said the Head, "I will give you my answer. You have no right to expect me to send you back to Kansas unless you do something for me in return. Help me and I will help you."

"What must I do?" asked the girl.

"Kill the Wicked Witch of the West," answered Oz.

"But I cannot!" exclaimed Dorothy, greatly surprised.

"You killed the Witch of the East and you wear the Silver Shoes, which bear a powerful charm. There is now but one Wicked Witch left in all this land, and when you can tell me she is dead I will send you back to Kansas—but not before."

Sorrowfully, Dorothy left the Throne Room and went back where her friends were waiting to hear what Oz had said to her. "There is no hope for me," she said sadly, "for Oz will not send me home until I have killed the Wicked Witch of the West—and that I can never do."

Next, the soldier with the green whiskers came to the Scarecrow, the Tin Woodman, and the Lion and said, "Come with me, for Oz has sent for you."

So they followed him and were admitted into the great Throne Room, where they were surprised to find that before the throne was a Ball of Fire, so fierce and glowing they could scarcely bear to gaze upon it.

Then a low, quiet voice came from the Ball of Fire, and these were the words it spoke:

"I am Oz, the Great and Terrible. Who are you, and why do you seek me?"

The Scarecrow stepped forward and said, "I am only a Scarecrow, stuffed with straw. Therefore I have no brains, and I come to you praying that you will put brains in my head instead of straw, so that I may become as wise as any other man."

Next, the Tin Woodman spoke up. "I am a Woodman, and made of tin. Therefore I have no heart, and cannot love. I pray you to give me a heart that I may be as other men are."

And the Lion answered, "I am a Cowardly Lion, afraid of everything. I come to you to beg that you give me courage, so that I may truly become the King of Beasts, as men call me."

"Why should I grant you these things?" said Oz.

"Because of all Wizards you are the greatest, and alone have power to grant our requests," answered the Lion.

The Ball of Fire burned fiercely for a time and the voice said, "I never grant favors without some return, but this much I will promise. If you will kill for me the Wicked Witch of the West, I will bestow upon you a great many brains, a kind, loving heart, and the courage you seek."

"I thought you asked Dorothy to kill the Witch," said the Scarecrow in surprise.

"I don't care who kills her! But until she is dead I will not grant your wishes. Now go, and do not seek me again until you have earned what you so greatly desire!"

The Lion was angry at this speech, but could say nothing in reply, and while he stood silently gazing at the Ball of Fire, it became so furiously hot that he turned tail and rushed from the room—his comrades close behind.

They told Dorothy of the Wizard's command.
"What shall we do now?" asked Dorothy sadly.

"There is only one thing we can do,"
returned the Lion, "and that is to leave tomorrow
to seek out the Wicked Witch, and destroy her."

CHAPTER TEN

The Search for the Wicked Witch

At daylight, our friends started toward the West, walking over fields of soft grass dotted here and there with daisies and buttercups. The Emerald City was soon left far behind.

Now, the Wicked Witch of the West had but one eye, yet that eye was as powerful as a telescope and could see everywhere. So, as she sat in the door of her yellow castle, she happened to look around, and she saw Dorothy with her friends. They were a long distance off, but the Wicked Witch was angry to find them in her country, so she blew upon a silver whistle that hung around her neck.

At once there came running to her from all directions a pack of great wolves. They had long legs and fierce eyes and sharp teeth.

"Go to those people," said the Witch, "and tear them to pieces."

"Very well," said the leader of the wolves. He dashed away at full speed, followed by the others.

It was lucky the Scarecrow and the Woodman heard the wolves coming.

"This is my fight," said the Woodman, "so get behind me and I will meet them as they come."

He seized his axe, and, as the leader of the wolves came on, the Tin Woodman swung his arm and chopped the wolf, so that it immediately died. There were forty wolves, and forty times a wolf was killed, so that at last they all lay dead in a heap before the Woodman.

The next morning, the Wicked Witch came to the door of her castle and looked out with her one eye. She saw all her wolves lying dead and the strangers still traveling through her country. This made her angrier than before. She blew her silver whistle *twice*.

Straightway a great flock of wild crows came flying toward her—enough to darken the sky.

The Wicked Witch said to the King Crow, "Fly at once to the strangers! Peck at them and tear them to pieces."

The wild crows flew in one great flock toward Dorothy and her companions. When the little girl saw them coming she was afraid.

But the Scarecrow said, "This is my battle, so lie down beside me and you will not be harmed."

The Scarecrow stretched out his arms. When the crows saw him they were frightened (as these birds always are by scarecrows).

But the King Crow said, "It is only a stuffed man. I will peck at him!"

The King Crow flew at the Scarecrow, who caught it by the head and killed it. There were forty crows, and forty times the Scarecrow caught and killed one, until at last all were lying dead beside him. Then he called to his companions to rise, and again they went upon their journey.

When the Wicked Witch looked out again and saw all her crows lying in a heap, she got into a terrible rage, and blew *three* times upon her silver whistle.

Soon there was heard a great buzzing in the air, and a swarm of black bees came flying toward her.

"Go to the strangers and sting them to death!" commanded the Witch, and the bees turned and flew rapidly until they came to where Dorothy and her friends were walking. But the Woodman had seen them coming, and he instructed the others to hide.

The bees came and found no one but the Woodman to sting, so they flew at him and broke off all their stings against the tin. And since bees cannot live when their stings are broken, that was the end of the black bees. They lay scattered thick about the Woodman like little heaps of fine coal.

The Wicked Witch was so angry when she saw her black bees in little heaps that she stamped her foot and tore her hair and gnashed her teeth. And then she called a dozen of her slaves, who were the yellow Winkies. She gave them sharp spears, telling them to go to the strangers and destroy them.

The Winkies were not a brave people, but they had to do as they were told. So they marched away until they came near to Dorothy. Then the Lion gave a great roar and sprang toward them, and the poor Winkies were so frightened that they ran back as fast as they could.

The Wicked Witch could not understand how all her plans to destroy these strangers had failed. She was a powerful Witch, as well as a wicked one, and she soon made up her mind how to act.

There was, in her cupboard, a Golden Cap, with a circle of diamonds and rubies running round it. This Golden Cap had a charm. Whoever owned it could call three times upon the Winged Monkeys, who would obey any order they were given. Only once more could she use this Golden Cap. But she saw there was only one way left to destroy Dorothy and her friends.

So the Wicked Witch took the Golden Cap from her cupboard and placed it upon her head. Then she stood upon her left foot and said slowly:
"Ep-pe, pep-pe, kak-ke!"
Next she stood upon her right foot and said:
"Hil-lo, hol-lo, hel-lo!"

After this she stood upon both feet and cried in a loud voice:

"*Ziz-zy, zuz-zy, zik!*"

Now the charm began to work. The sky was darkened and a low rumbling sound was heard in the air. There was a rushing of many wings, a great chattering and laughing. The sun came out of the dark sky to show the Wicked Witch surrounded by a crowd of monkeys, each with a pair of large, powerful wings on his shoulders.

One, much bigger than the others, seemed to be their leader. He flew close to the Witch and said, "You have called us for the third and last time. What do you command?"

"Go to the strangers who are within my land and destroy them all except the Lion," said the Wicked Witch. "Bring that beast to me, for I have a mind to harness him like a horse and make him work."

"Your commands shall be obeyed," said the leader. Then, with a great deal of noise, the Winged Monkeys flew away to the place where Dorothy and her friends were walking.

Some of the Monkeys seized the Tin Woodman and carried him through the air until

they were over a country thickly covered with sharp rocks. Here they dropped the poor Woodman, who fell a great distance to the rocks. He lay so battered and dented that he could neither move nor groan.

Other Monkeys caught the Scarecrow, and, with their long fingers, pulled all of the straw out of his clothes and head. They made his hat and boots and clothes into a small bundle and threw it into the top branches of a tall tree.

The remaining Monkeys threw pieces of stout rope around the Lion and then they lifted him up and flew away with him to the Witch's castle. There he was placed in a small yard with a high iron fence around it, so that he could not escape.

But they did not harm Dorothy at all. She stood, with Toto in her arms, watching the sad fate of her comrades and thinking it would soon be her turn.

"We dare not harm this little girl," the leader of the Winged Monkeys said, "for she has the mark of the Good Witch's kiss and is protected by the Power of Good, which is greater than the Power of Evil. All we can do is carry her to the

castle of the Wicked Witch and leave her there."

So, carefully and gently, they lifted Dorothy in their arms and carried her swiftly through the air until they came to the castle, where they set her down upon the front doorstep. Then the leader said to the Witch, "We have obeyed you as far as we were able. The Tin Woodman and the Scarecrow are destroyed, and the Lion is tied up in your yard. The little girl we dare not harm, nor the dog she carries in her arms. Your power over us is now ended and you will never see us again."

Then all the Winged Monkeys, with much laughing and chattering and noise, flew into the air and were soon out of sight.

The Wicked Witch was both surprised and worried when she saw the mark on Dorothy's forehead, for she knew she dare not hurt the girl in any way. She looked down at Dorothy's feet. Seeing the Silver Shoes, she began to tremble with fear, for she knew what a powerful charm belonged to them. At first the Witch was tempted to run away from Dorothy, but she happened to look into the child's eyes and saw she had a simple soul. The little girl did not know of the wonderful power of the Silver Shoes. The Wicked Witch laughed to herself and thought, "I can still make her my slave, for she does not know how to use her power."

She said to Dorothy, harshly, "Come with me! See that you mind everything I tell you. For if you do not, I will make an end of you, as I did of the Tin Woodman and the Scarecrow."

Dorothy followed her through many of the beautiful rooms in her castle until they came to

the kitchen, where the Witch made her clean the pots and kettles and sweep the floor and keep the fire fed with wood.

Now the Wicked Witch wanted the Silver Shoes, which the girl always wore, and she finally thought of a trick to get them. She placed a bar of iron in the middle of the kitchen floor, and then by her magic arts made the iron invisible to human eyes. When Dorothy walked across the floor she stumbled over the bar, not being able to see it, and fell at full length. She was not much hurt, but in her fall one of the Silver Shoes came off. Before she could reach it, the Witch had snatched it away and put it on her own skinny foot.

The wicked woman was greatly pleased with the success of her trick, for as long as she had one of the shoes she owned half the power of their charm, and Dorothy could not use it against her, even had she known how to do so.

The little girl, seeing she had lost one of her pretty shoes, grew angry, and said to the Witch, "Give me back my shoe!"

"I will not," screamed the Witch, "for it is now my shoe, and not yours."

"You are a wicked creature!" cried Dorothy. "You have no right to take my shoe from me."

"I shall keep it, just the same," said the Witch, laughing, "and someday I shall get the other one from you, too."

This made Dorothy so very angry that she picked up the bucket of water that stood near and dashed it over the Witch, wetting her from head to foot.

Instantly the wicked woman gave a loud cry of fear, and then, as Dorothy looked at her in wonder, the Witch began to shrink and fall away.

"See what you have done!" she screamed. "In a minute I shall melt away."

"I'm very sorry, indeed," said Dorothy, who was truly frightened to see the Witch actually melting away like brown sugar before her very eyes.

"Didn't you know water would be the end of me?" asked the Witch, in a wailing, despairing voice.

"Of course not," answered Dorothy. "How could I?"

"Well, in a few minutes I shall be all melted, and you will have the castle to yourself. I have been wicked in my day, but I never thought

a little girl like you would ever be able to melt me and end my wicked deeds. Look out— here I go!"

Soon, all that was left was a brown puddle and one Silver Shoe.

CHAPTER ELEVEN

The Rescue

The Cowardly Lion was much pleased to hear that the Wicked Witch had been melted by a bucket of water, and Dorothy at once unlocked the gate of his prison and set him free. They went together into the yellow castle, where Dorothy's first act was to call all the Winkies together and tell them that they were no longer slaves.

There was great rejoicing among the yellow Winkies, for they had been made to work hard during many years for the Wicked Witch, who had always treated them with great cruelty. They kept this day as a holiday, then and ever after, and spent the time in feasting and dancing.

"If our friends the Scarecrow and the Tin Woodman were only with us," said the Lion, "I should be quite happy."

"Don't you suppose we could rescue them?" asked the girl anxiously.

"We can try," answered the Lion.

So they called the yellow Winkies and asked them if they would help to rescue their friends. The Winkies said that they would be delighted to do all in their power for Dorothy. So she chose a number of the Winkies and they all started away. They traveled that day and part of the next until they came to the rocky plain where the Tin Woodman lay, all battered and bent.

The Winkies lifted him tenderly in their arms and carried him back to the yellow castle, where they worked for three days and four nights, hammering and twisting and bending and polishing and pounding at the legs and body and head of the Tin Woodman. At last he was straightened out into his old form, and his joints worked as well as ever.

"If we only had the Scarecrow with us again," said the Tin Woodman, when Dorothy had finished telling him everything that had happened, "I should be quite happy."

"We must try to find him," said the girl.

So she called the Winkies to help her, and they walked all that day and part of the next until they came to the tall tree that held the Scarecrow's clothes.

It was a very tall tree, and the trunk was so smooth that no one could climb it. The Woodman said at once, "I'll chop it down, and then we can get the Scarecrow's clothes."

In a short time the tree fell over with a crash, whereupon all the Scarecrow's clothes fell out of the branches and rolled onto the ground.

Dorothy picked them up and had the Winkies carry them back to the castle, where they were stuffed with nice, clean straw—and behold! Here was the Scarecrow, as good as ever, thanking them over and over again for saving him.

Now that they were reunited, Dorothy and her friends spent a few happy days at the Yellow Castle, where they found everything they needed to make them comfortable.

But one day the girl thought of Aunt Em, and said, "We must go back to Oz, and claim his promise."

"Yes," said the Woodman, "at last I shall get my heart."

"And I shall get my brains," added the Scarecrow joyfully.

"And I shall get my courage," said the Lion thoughtfully.

"And I shall get back to Kansas," cried Dorothy, clapping her hands. "Oh, let us start for the Emerald City tomorrow!"

This they decided to do.

◆ ◆ ◆

The next day they called the Winkies together and said good-bye. The Winkies were sorry to have them go. They had grown so fond of the Tin Woodman that they begged him to stay and rule over them and the Yellow Land of the West. Finding they were determined to go, the Winkies gave Toto and the Lion each a golden collar. To Dorothy they presented a beautiful bracelet studded with diamonds. To the Scarecrow they gave a gold-headed walking stick, to keep him from stumbling. To the Tin Woodman they offered a silver oil can, inlaid with gold and set with precious jewels.

Dorothy went to the Witch's cupboard to fill her basket with food for the journey, and there she saw the Golden Cap. She tried it on her own head and found that it fitted her exactly.

She did not know anything about the charm of the Golden Cap, but she saw that it was pretty,

so she made up her mind to wear it, and carry her sunbonnet in the basket.

Then, being prepared for the journey, they all started for the Emerald City. The Winkies gave them three cheers and many good wishes to carry with them.

CHAPTER TWELVE

The Winged Monkeys

You will remember there was no road—not even a pathway—between the castle of the Wicked Witch and the Emerald City. They knew, of course, they must go straight east, toward the rising sun. They started off in the right way, but at noon, when the sun was over their heads, they did not know which was east and which was west. They were lost in the great fields.

"If we walk far enough," said Dorothy, "I am sure we shall sometime come to some place."

But day by day passed away, and they still saw nothing before them but the scarlet fields. The Scarecrow began to grumble a bit.

"We have surely lost our way," he said, "and unless we find it again in time to reach the Emerald City, I shall never get my brains."

"Nor I my heart," declared the Tin Woodman.

"You see," said the Cowardly Lion, with a whimper, "I haven't the courage to keep tramping forever, without getting anywhere at all."

"Suppose we call the field mice," Dorothy suggested. "They could probably tell us the way to the Emerald City."

"To be sure they could," cried the Scarecrow. "Why didn't we think of that before?"

Dorothy blew the little whistle the Queen of the Field Mice had given her. In a few minutes they heard the pattering of tiny feet, and many of the small gray mice came running up to her. Among them was the Queen herself, who asked, in her squeaky little voice, "What can I do for my friends?"

"We have lost our way," said Dorothy. "Can you tell us where the Emerald City is?"

"Certainly," answered the Queen, "but it is a great way off." Then she noticed Dorothy's Golden Cap. "Why don't you use the charm of the Cap, and call the Winged Monkeys? They will carry you to the City of Oz in less than an hour."

"I didn't know there was a charm," answered Dorothy, in surprise. "What is it?"

"It is written inside the Golden Cap," replied the Queen of the Field Mice, "but the wearer of the Cap may use the charm only three times." Here the Queen curtsied. "If you are going to call the Winged Monkeys, we must run away—for they are full of mischief and think it great fun to tease us."

"Won't they hurt me?" asked the girl.

"Oh, no," said the mouse. "They must obey the wearer of the Cap. Good-bye!" And she scampered out of sight, with all the mice hurrying after her.

Dorothy looked inside the Golden Cap and saw some words written upon the lining. These, she thought, must be the charm, so she read the directions carefully and put the Cap upon her head.

"*Ep-pe, pep-pe, kak-ke!*" she said, standing on her left foot.

"*Hil-lo, hol-lo, hel-lo!*" Dorothy went on, standing this time on her right foot.

"*Ziz-zy, zuz-zy, zik!*" said Dorothy, standing on both feet.

Suddenly they heard a great chattering and flapping of wings, as the band of Winged Monkeys flew up to Dorothy. The King bowed low and asked, "What is your command?"

"We wish to go to the Emerald City," said the child, "and we have lost our way."

"We will carry you," replied the King. No sooner had he spoken than two Monkeys caught Dorothy in their arms and flew away with her. Others took the Scarecrow, the Woodman, and the Lion, and one little Monkey seized Toto and flew after them.

Dorothy found herself riding easily between two of the biggest Monkeys, one of them the King himself. They had made a chair of their hands and were careful not to hurt her.

After a long journey, Dorothy looked down and saw the green, shining walls of the Emerald City before them. The strange creatures set the travelers down carefully before the gate of the City. The King bowed low to Dorothy, and then flew swiftly away, followed by all his band.

"That was a good ride," said the little girl.

"Yes, and a quick way out of our troubles," replied the Lion. "How lucky it was you brought away that wonderful Cap!"

CHAPTER THIRTEEN

The Discovery of Oz, The Terrible

The four travelers walked up to the great gate of the Emerald City and rang the bell. After ringing several times, it was opened by the same Guardian of the Gates they had met before.

"What! Are you back again?" he asked in surprise.

"Do you not see us?" answered the Scarecrow.

"But I thought you had gone to visit the Wicked Witch of the West."

"We did visit her," said the Scarecrow.

"And she let you go?" asked the man, in wonder.

"She could not help it, for she is melted," explained the Scarecrow.

"Melted! Well, that is good news, indeed,"

said the man. "Who melted her?"

"It was Dorothy," said the Lion proudly.

"Good gracious!" exclaimed the man, and he bowed very low indeed. Then he fitted them with their green eyeglasses and led them through the gate into the Emerald City. When the people heard that Dorothy had melted the Wicked Witch of the West, they all gathered around the travelers and followed them to the Palace of Oz.

The soldier with the green whiskers was still on guard before the door, but he let them in at once, and they were again met by the beautiful green girl, who showed each of them to their old rooms at once, so they might rest until the Great Oz was ready to receive them.

Promptly at nine o'clock the next morning they all went into the Throne Room of the Great Oz.

Before long, they heard a deep Voice that seemed to come from somewhere near the top of the great dome, and it said:

"I am Oz, the Great and Terrible. Why do you seek me?"

"We have come to claim our promise, Great Oz."

"Is the Wicked Witch really destroyed?" asked the Voice, and Dorothy thought it trembled a little.

"Yes," she answered. "I melted her with a bucket of water."

"Dear me," said the Voice. "How sudden! Well, come to me tomorrow, for I must have time to think it over."

"You've had plenty of time already," said the Tin Woodman angrily.

"We shan't wait a day longer," said the Scarecrow.

"You must keep your promises to us!" exclaimed Dorothy.

The Lion thought it might do well to frighten the Wizard, so he gave a large, loud roar. It was so fierce and dreadful that Toto jumped away from him in alarm and tipped over the screen that stood in a corner. As it fell with a crash, they saw, standing in just the spot the screen had hidden, a little old man with a bald head and a wrinkled face, who seemed to be as surprised as they were.

The Tin Woodman, raising his axe, rushed toward the little man and cried out, "Who are you?"

"I am Oz, the Great and Terrible," said the little man, in a trembling voice. "But don't hurt me—please don't—and I'll do anything you want."

Our friends looked at him in surprise and dismay.

"I thought Oz was a great Head," said Dorothy.

"And I thought Oz was a Ball of Fire," exclaimed the Lion.

"No, you are wrong," said the little man meekly. "I have been making believe."

"Making believe!" cried Dorothy. "Are you not a Great Wizard?"

"Not a bit of it, my dear. I'm just a common man."

"You're more than that," said the Scarecrow, angry and confused. "You're a *humbug*!"

"Exactly so!" declared the little man, rubbing his hands together. "I *am* a humbug."

"Does anyone else know you're a humbug?" asked Dorothy.

"No one knows it but you four—and myself," replied Oz. "I have fooled everyone so long that I thought I would never be found out. It was a great mistake letting you into the Throne Room. Usually I will not see even my subjects, and so they believe I am something terrible."

"Really," said the Scarecrow, "you ought to be ashamed of yourself for being such a humbug."

"I am—I certainly am," answered the little man sorrowfully, "but it was the only thing I could do. Sit down, please, there are plenty of chairs. I will tell you my story."

So they sat down and listened while he told the following tale.

"I was born in Omaha…"

"Why, that isn't very far from Kansas!" cried Dorothy.

"No, but it is very *very* far from here," he said, shaking his head at her sadly. "When I grew up I became a balloonist."

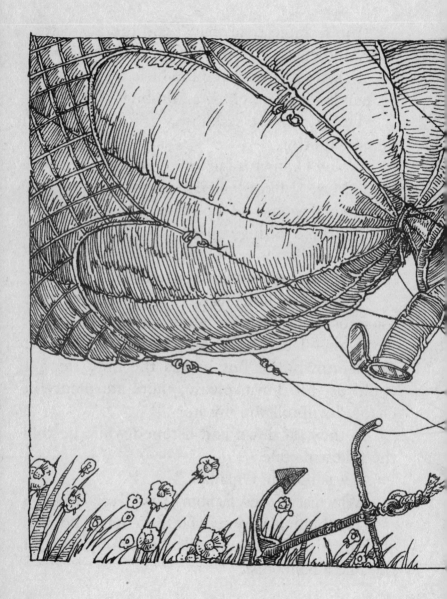

"What is that?" asked Dorothy.

"A man who goes up in a balloon on circus day, so as to draw a crowd of people together and get them to pay to see the circus," he explained.

"Oh," she said, "I know."

"Well, one day I went up in a balloon and the ropes got twisted, so that I couldn't come down again. It went way up above the clouds, and the wind carried it many, many miles away.

"It came down slowly and I was not hurt a bit. But I found myself in the midst of a strange people, who, seeing me come from the clouds, thought I was a great Wizard. Of course I let them think so, because they were afraid of me and they promised to do anything that I wished them to do.

"Just to amuse myself, and keep the good people busy, I ordered them to build this City and my Palace. They did it all willingly and well. Then I thought, as the country was so green and beautiful, I would call it the Emerald City. I have been good to the people, and they like me. But ever since this Palace was built, I have shut myself up and would not see any of them.

"My greatest fear was of the Witches of the East and West, for they were terribly wicked. They thought I was powerful and terrible, so they left me alone. Still, I lived in deadly fear of them for many years. So you can imagine how pleased I was when I heard your house had fallen on the Wicked Witch of the East. When you came to me, I was willing to promise anything if you would only do away with the other Witch. But now that you have melted her, I am ashamed to say that I cannot keep my promises."

"I think you are a very bad man," said Dorothy.

"Oh, no, my dear. I'm really a very good man, but I'm a very bad Wizard, I must admit."

"Can't you give me brains?" asked the Scarecrow.

"You don't need them. You are learning something every day. A baby has brains, but it doesn't know much. Experience is the only thing that brings knowledge, and the longer you are on earth the more experience you are sure to get."

"That may all be true," said the Scarecrow, "but I shall be very unhappy unless you give me brains."

The false Wizard looked at him carefully.

The Wizard unfastened the Scarecrow's head and emptied out the straw. Then he entered the

back room and took up a measure of bran, which he mixed with a great many pins and needles. He shook all this together and then filled the top of the Scarecrow's head with the mixture and stuffed the rest of the space with straw—to hold it in place.

When he had fastened the Scarecrow's head on his body again he said to him, "Hereafter you will be a great man, for I have given you a lot of *bran-new* brains."

The Scarecrow was both pleased and proud that his wish was granted. He thanked Oz warmly and then he turned to his friends.

Dorothy looked at him curiously. His head was quite lumpy and it bulged out at the top with brains.

"How do you feel?" she asked.

"I feel wise indeed," he answered. "When I get used to my brains I shall know everything."

"Why are those needles and pins sticking out of your head?" asked the Tin Woodman.

"That is proof that he is sharp," remarked the Lion.

"How about my heart?" asked the Tin Woodman.

"Why, as for that," answered Oz, "I think you are wrong to want a heart. It makes most people unhappy. If you only knew it, you are in luck not to have a heart."

"That may be how *you* feel," said the Tin Woodman, "but for my part, I will bear all the unhappiness without a murmur—if you will give me the heart."

"Very well," answered Oz. He brought out a pair of tinsmith's shears and cut a small, square hole in the left side of the Tin Woodman's chest. Then, going to a dresser drawer, he took out a pretty heart, made entirely of silk and stuffed with sawdust.

"Isn't it a beauty?" he asked.

"It is, indeed!" replied the Woodman, who was greatly pleased. "But is it a kind heart?"

"Oh, very!" answered Oz. He put the heart in the Woodman's chest and then replaced the square of tin.

The happy Woodman exclaimed, "I am very grateful to you, and shall never forget your kindness."

"You are most welcome," replied Oz.

"How about my courage?" asked the Lion.

"You have plenty of courage, I am sure," answered Oz. "All you need is confidence in yourself. There is no living thing that is not afraid when it faces danger. *True* courage is shown by facing danger when you are afraid, and that kind of courage you have in plenty."

"Perhaps I have, but I'm scared just the same," said the Lion. "I shall really be very unhappy unless you give me the sort of courage that makes one forget he is afraid."

"Very well," replied Oz. "I will get it for you."

He went to a cupboard and reaching up to a high shelf took down a square, green bottle. He poured a liquid into a green-gold dish, beautifully carved. Placing this before the Cowardly Lion, who sniffed at it as if he did not like it, the Wizard said, "Drink."

"What is it?" asked the Lion.

"Well," answered Oz, "if it were inside of you, it would be courage. You know, of course, that courage is always *inside* a person, so this really cannot be called courage until you have swallowed it. Therefore I advise you to drink it as soon as possible."

The Lion hesitated no longer, but drank till the dish was empty.

"How do you feel now?" asked Oz.

"Full of courage," replied the Lion, thanking him.

"And now," said Dorothy, "how am I to get back to Kansas?"

"We shall have to think about that," replied the little man. "Give me two or three days to consider the matter and I'll try to find a way to carry you over the desert. In the meantime you shall all be treated as my guests, and while you live in the Palace my people will wait upon you and obey your slightest wish. There is only one thing I ask in return for my help—such as it is. You must keep my secret and tell no one I am a humbug."

They agreed to say nothing of what they had learned, and went back to their rooms in high spirits.

Oz, left to himself, smiled to think of his success in giving the Scarecrow and the Tin Woodman and the Lion exactly what they thought they wanted.

"How can I help being a humbug," he said,

"when all these people make me do things that everybody knows can't be done? It was easy to make the Scarecrow and the Lion and the Woodman happy, because they imagined I could do anything. But it will take more than imagination to carry Dorothy back to Kansas. I'm sure I don't know how it can be done."

CHAPTER FOURTEEN

How the Balloon Was Launched

After four days, to her great joy, Oz sent for Dorothy, and when she entered the Throne Room he greeted her pleasantly.

"Sit down, my dear. I think I have found the way to get you out of this country."

"And back to Kansas?" she asked eagerly.

"Well, I'm not sure about Kansas," said Oz, "for I haven't the faintest notion which way it lies. But the first thing to do is to cross the desert, and then it should be easy to find your way home."

"How can I cross the desert?" she inquired.

"Well, I'll tell you what I think," said the little man. "You see, when I came to this country it was

in a balloon. You also came through the air, being carried by a cyclone. So I believe the best way to get across the desert will be through the air. Now, it is quite beyond my powers to make a cyclone, but I've been thinking the matter over, and I believe I can make a balloon for us."

"Us!" exclaimed the girl. "Are you going, too?"

"Yes, of course," replied Oz. "I am tired of being such a humbug. If I should go out of this Palace, my people would soon discover I am not a Wizard, and then they would be angry with me for having lied to them. So I have to stay shut up in these rooms all day, and it gets tiresome. I'd much rather go back to Kansas with you and be in a circus again."

"I shall be glad to have your company," said Dorothy.

After many days and much work, the great balloon was ready, and Oz ordered that it be carried out in front of the Palace. The people gazed upon it with much curiosity.

Then Oz got into the basket and said to all the people in a loud voice, "I am now going away to make a visit. While I am gone the Scarecrow will rule over you. I command you to obey him as you would me. Come, Dorothy!" he cried. "Hurry up, or the balloon will fly away."

"I can't find Toto anywhere," replied Dorothy, who did not wish to leave her little dog behind. Toto had run into the crowd to bark at a kitten, and Dorothy at last found him. She picked him up and ran toward the balloon.

She was within a few steps of it, and Oz was holding out his hands to help her into the basket, when *crack!* went the ropes, and the balloon rose into the air without her.

"Come back!" she screamed. "I want to go, too!"

"I can't come back, my dear," called Oz from the basket. "Good-bye!"

"Good-bye!" shouted everyone, and all eyes were turned upward to where the Wizard was riding in the basket, rising every moment farther and farther into the sky.

And that was the last any of them ever saw of Oz, the Wonderful Wizard. But the people remembered him lovingly, and said to one another, "Oz was always our friend. When he was here he built for us this beautiful Emerald City. Now he is gone, but he has left the Wise Scarecrow to rule over us."

CHAPTER FIFTEEN

Away to the South

Dorothy wept bitterly. She had lost her last chance to get home to Kansas again. The morning after the balloon had gone up with Oz, Dorothy and her three companions met in the Throne Room and talked matters over. The Scarecrow sat in the big throne and the others stood respectfully before him.

"We are not so unlucky," said the new ruler, "for this Palace and the Emerald City belong to us, and we can do just as we please."

"But I don't want to live here," cried Dorothy. "I want to live with Aunt Em and Uncle Henry."

"Well, what can be done?" asked the Woodman.

The Scarecrow decided to think, and he thought so hard that the pins and needles began to stick out of his brains. Finally he said, "Why not call the Winged Monkeys, and ask them to carry you over the desert?"

"I never thought of that!" said Dorothy joyfully. "I'll go at once for the Golden Cap."

When she brought it into the Throne Room she spoke the magic words, and soon the band of Winged Monkeys flew in through the open window and stood beside her.

"This is the second time you have called us," said the Monkey King, bowing before the little girl. "What do you wish?"

"I want you to fly with me to Kansas," Dorothy said.

"That cannot be done," he said. "We belong to this country alone, and cannot leave it. There has never been a Winged Monkey in Kansas yet, and I suppose there never will be, for they don't belong there. We shall be glad to serve you, but we cannot cross the desert. Good-bye."

The Scarecrow was thinking again. "Let us call in the soldier with the green whiskers," he said, "and ask his advice."

So the soldier was summoned and entered the Throne Room timidly, for while Oz was alive he never was allowed to come farther than the door.

"This little girl," said the Scarecrow to the soldier, "wishes to cross the desert. How can she do so?"

"I cannot tell," answered the soldier, "for nobody has ever crossed the desert, unless it is Oz himself."

"Is there no one who can help me?" asked Dorothy earnestly.

"Glinda might," he suggested.

"Who is Glinda?" inquired the Scarecrow.

"The Good Witch of the South. She is the most powerful of all the Witches, and rules over the Quadlings. Besides, her castle stands on the edge of the desert, so she may know a way to cross it."

"How can I get to her castle?" asked Dorothy.

"The road is straight to the South," he answered, "but it is said to be full of dangers to travelers. There are wild beasts in the woods, and a tribe of odd men who do not like strangers to cross their country. For this reason none of the Quadlings ever come to the Emerald City."

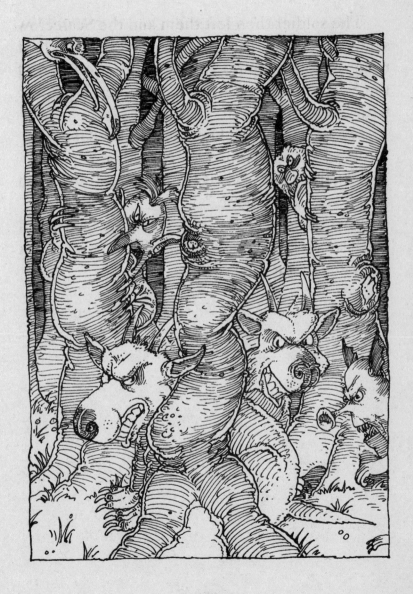

The soldier then left them and the Scarecrow said, "It seems, in spite of dangers, that the best thing Dorothy can do is to travel to the Land of the South and ask Glinda to help her. I shall go with Dorothy."

"I too shall go with Dorothy," declared the Lion.

"And I!" proclaimed the Woodman.

"Thank you," said Dorothy gratefully. "You are all very kind to me."

"We shall go tomorrow morning," returned the Scarecrow. "So now let us all get ready, for it will be a long journey."

CHAPTER SIXTEEN

The Journey to the Country of the Quadlings

The next morning, the sun shone brightly as our friends turned their faces toward the Land of the South. They were all in the best of spirits, and laughed and chatted together. Dorothy was once more filled with the hope of getting home, and the Scarecrow and the Tin Woodman were glad to be of use to her. As for the Lion, he sniffed the fresh air with delight and whisked his tail from side to side in pure joy at being in the country again, while Toto ran around them and chased the moths and butterflies, barking merrily all the time.

The first day's journey was through the green fields and bright flowers that stretched about the Emerald City on every side, but the days that followed brought many dangerous adventures for the travelers.

In the morning of their second day, they came to a thick wood filled with trees as far as they could see. They discovered these trees had wide-spreading branches that reached out and grabbed them, flinging them to the ground. The Woodman saved his companions by fiercely chopping at the fighting limbs, making a path that they might pass.

Then the travelers found themselves in a wild-looking forest where the trees were bigger and older than any they had ever seen.

"This forest is perfectly delightful," declared the Lion, looking around him with joy. "Never have I seen a more beautiful place."

"It seems gloomy," said the Scarecrow.

"Not a bit," answered the Lion. "I would like to live here all my life. Surely no wild beast could wish for a more pleasant home."

"Perhaps there are wild beasts in the forest now," said Dorothy.

"I suppose there are," returned the Lion.

The following morning, they came to an opening in the wood, in which there were gathered hundreds of animals of every variety. There were tigers and elephants and bears and wolves and foxes, among others, and for a moment Dorothy was afraid. But the Lion explained that the animals were holding a meeting, and he judged by their snarling and growling that they were in great trouble.

As he spoke, several of the beasts caught sight of him. The biggest of the tigers came up to the Lion and bowed. "Welcome, O King of Beasts!"

the tiger said. "You have come at a good time to fight our enemy and bring peace to all the animals of the forest once more."

"What is your trouble?" asked the Lion quietly.

"We are all threatened," answered the tiger, "by a fierce enemy which has lately come into this forest. It is a most tremendous monster, like a great spider, with a body as big as an elephant and legs as long as a tree trunk. Not one of us is safe while this fierce creature is alive, and we had called a meeting to decide how to take care of ourselves when you came among us."

"If I put an end to your enemy, will you bow down to me and obey me as King of the Forest?" asked the Lion.

"We will do that gladly," returned the tiger. All the other beasts roared with a mighty roar: "We will!"

So, the Lion said good-bye to his friends and marched proudly away to do battle with the enemy.

The great spider was lying asleep when the Lion found him, and it looked so ugly that the Lion turned up his nose in disgust. Its legs were quite as long as the tiger had said, and its body was covered with coarse black hair. The Lion knew it was easier to fight it asleep than awake,

so he gave a great spring and landed directly upon the monster's back. Then, with one blow of his heavy paw, he killed the monster.

The Lion went back to where the beasts of the forest were waiting for him and said proudly, "You need fear your enemy no longer."

Then the beasts bowed down to the Lion as their King, and he promised to come back and rule over them as soon as Dorothy was safely on her way to Kansas.

The four travelers passed through the rest of the forest in safety, and when they came out from its gloom they saw before them a steep hill, covered from top to bottom with great pieces of rock.

"That will be a hard climb," said the Scarecrow.

They had nearly reached the first rock when they discovered hundreds of the strangest men the travelers had ever seen. These men had big, flat heads and necks full of wrinkles. They had no arms at all but were dangerous just the same. As the travelers tried to pass, the armless Hammer-Heads shot forward. Their necks stretched out until the tops of their flat heads *struck!*—sending their enemy rolling down the hill as if hit by cannon balls.

They realized it was useless to fight the people with the shooting heads, so Dorothy called the Winged Monkeys one last time. Putting on the Golden Cap, she uttered the magic words. In moments, the Monkeys stood before her.

"What are your commands?" inquired the King of the Monkeys, bowing low.

"Carry us over the hill to the country of the Quadlings," answered the girl.

Then, before the Hammer-Heads could do more damage, the King said, "It shall be done," and at once the Winged Monkeys caught the four travelers and Toto up in their arms and flew away with them. As they passed over the hill the Hammer-Heads yelled with anger, and shot their heads high in the air at them, but they could not reach them. The Winged Monkeys carried Dorothy and her comrades safely over the hill and set them down in the beautiful country of the Quadlings.

"This is the last time you can call us," said the leader to Dorothy. "So, good-bye and good luck to you."

"Good-bye and thank you very much," returned the girl.

The Winged Monkeys rose into the air and were out of sight in a twinkling.

The country of the Quadlings seemed rich and happy. Dorothy and her friends walked by fields and across pretty bridges until they saw before them a very beautiful Castle. Before the gates were three young girls, dressed in handsome red uniforms trimmed with gold braid. As Dorothy approached, one of them said to her, "Why have you come to the South Country?"

"To see the Good Witch who rules here," she answered. "Will you take me to her?"

"Let me have your name, and I will ask Glinda if she will receive you." They told who they were, and the girl soldier went into the Castle. After a few moments she came back to say that Dorothy and the others were to be admitted at once.

CHAPTER SEVENTEEN

Glinda the Good Witch Grants Dorothy's Wish

They followed the soldier girl into a big room where the Witch Glinda sat upon a throne of rubies.

She was both beautiful and young to their eyes. Her hair was a rich red color and fell in flowing curls over her shoulders. Her dress was pure white but her eyes were blue, and they looked kindly upon the little girl.

"What can I do for you, my child?" she asked.

Dorothy told the Witch all of her story: how the cyclone had brought her to the Land of Oz, how she had found her companions, and of the wonderful adventures they had met with.

"My greatest wish now," she added, "is to get back to Kansas, for Aunt Em will surely think something dreadful has happened to me."

"Bless your dear heart," Glinda said, "I am sure I can tell you of a way to get back to Kansas. But, if I do, you must give me the Golden Cap."

"Willingly!" exclaimed Dorothy. "Indeed, it is of no use to me now, and when you have it you can command the Winged Monkeys three times."

"And I think I shall need their service just those three times," answered Glinda, smiling.

Dorothy then gave her the Golden Cap, and the Witch said to the Scarecrow, "What will you do when Dorothy has left us?"

"I will return to the Emerald City," he replied, "for Oz has made me its ruler and the people like me. The only thing that worries me is how to cross the hill of the Hammer-Heads."

"By means of the Golden Cap I shall command the Winged Monkeys to carry you to the gates of the Emerald City," said Glinda, "for you will make a very wise ruler."

Turning to the Tin Woodman, she asked, "What will become of you when Dorothy leaves this country?"

He leaned on his axe and thought a moment. Then he said, "The Winkies were very kind to me, and wanted me to rule over them after the Wicked Witch died. I am fond of the Winkies, and if I could get back again to the Country of the West, I should like nothing better than to rule over them forever."

"My second command to the Winged Monkeys," said Glinda, "will be that they carry you safely to the land of the Winkies. I am sure you will care for the Winkies with all your heart."

Then the Witch looked at the big, shaggy Lion and asked, "When Dorothy has returned to her own home, what will become of you?"

"Over the hill of the Hammer-Heads," he answered, "lies a grand old forest, and all the beasts that live there have made me their King. If I could only get back to this forest, I would pass my life very happily there."

"My third command to the Winged Monkeys," said Glinda, "shall be to carry you to your forest to rule bravely. Then, having used up the powers of the Golden Cap, I shall give it to the King of the Monkeys, that he and his band may thereafter be free for ever more."

The Scarecrow and the Tin Woodman and the Lion now thanked the Good Witch for her kindness.

Then Dorothy exclaimed, "You are certainly as good as you are beautiful! But you have not yet told me how to get back to Kansas."

"Your Silver Shoes will carry you over the desert," replied Glinda. "If you had known their power you could have gone back to your Aunt Em the very first day you came to this country."

"But then I would not have had my wonderful brains!" cried the Scarecrow. "I might have passed my whole life in the farmer's cornfield."

"And I would not have had my lovely heart," said the Tin Woodman. "I might have stood and rusted in the forest till the end of the world."

"And I would have lived a coward forever," declared the Lion, "and no beast in all the forest would have had a good word to say to me."

"This is all true," said Dorothy, "and I am glad I was of use to these good friends. But now that each of them has what he most desires, and each is happy in having a kingdom to rule besides, I think I should like to go back to Kansas."

"The Silver Shoes," said the Good Witch, "have wonderful powers. All you have to do is click the heels together three times and command the shoes to carry you wherever you wish to go."

"If that is so," said the child joyfully, "I will ask them to carry me back to Kansas at once."

She threw her arms around the Lion's neck and kissed him, patting his big head tenderly.

Then she kissed the Tin Woodman, who was weeping in a way most dangerous to his joints. But she hugged the soft, stuffed body of the Scarecrow in her arms instead of kissing his painted face, and found she was crying herself at this sorrowful parting from her loving friends.

Dorothy now took Toto up in her arms, and, having said one last good-bye, she clicked the heels of her shoes together one—two—three times, saying, "Take me home to Aunt Em!"

Instantly she was whirling through the air *so swiftly* that all she could see or feel was the wind whistling past her ears. Then she stopped *so suddenly* that she rolled over upon the grass several times before she knew where she was. At length, however, she sat up and looked about her.

"Good gracious!" she cried.

For she was sitting on the broad Kansas prairie, and just before her was the new farmhouse Uncle Henry built after the cyclone had carried away the old one. Uncle Henry was milking the cows in the barnyard, and Toto had jumped out of her arms and was running toward the barn, barking furiously.

Dorothy stood up and found she was in her stocking-feet—for the Silver Shoes had fallen off in her flight through the air and were lost forever in the desert.

CHAPTER EIGHTEEN

Home Again

Aunt Em had just come out of the house to water the cabbages when she looked up and saw Dorothy running toward her.

"My darling child!" she cried, folding the little girl in her arms and covering her face with kisses. "Where in the world did you come from?"

"From the Land of Oz," exclaimed Dorothy, with wonder and joy. "And here is Toto, too. And oh, Aunt Em! I'm so glad to be at home again!"

THE END

L. FRANK BAUM

Lyman Frank Baum was born in 1856 in Chittenango, New York. He grew up on a lovely country estate called *Rose Lawn*. At an early age, Frank displayed an interest in writing and printing. His father bought him a printing press when Frank was fifteen—and from that day on, publishing became his focus.

After he married in 1882, he moved to South Dakota, where he published his own weekly newspaper, filled with news and his creative writings. In 1896, he moved his family to Chicago, where he wrote children's stories. His first book was called *Father Goose*, which was very successful. But it was his second book that made him—and Dorothy, Toto, and all the characters of Oz—famous around the world. *The Wonderful Wizard of Oz* was published in 1900. Baum dedicated the book "to my good friend and comrade—my wife."

L. Frank Baum went on to write about 60 children's books, including many more set in the Land of Oz. He died in 1919.